A Beginning-to-Read Book

Happy Easter, Dear Dragon

by Margaret Hillert

Illustrated by Carl Kock

NORWOOD HOUSE PRESS

DEAR CAREGIVER,

The *Beginning-to-Read* series is a carefully written collection of classic readers you may remember from your own childhood. Each book features text comprised of common sight words to provide your child ample practice reading the words that appear most frequently in written text. The many additional details in the pictures enhance the story and offer the opportunity for you to help your child expand oral language and develop comprehension.

Begin by reading the story to your child, followed by letting him or her read familiar words and soon your child will be able to read the story independently. At each step of the way, be sure to praise your reader's efforts to build his or her confidence as an independent reader. Discuss the pictures and encourage your child to make connections between the story and his or her own life. At the end of the story, you will find reading activities and a word list that will help your child practice and strengthen beginning reading skills.

Above all, the most important part of the reading experience is to have fun and enjoy it!

Shannon Cannon

Shannon Cannon,
Literacy Consultant

Norwood House Press • P.O. Box 316598 • Chicago, Illinois 60631
For more information about Norwood House Press please visit our website at
www.norwoodhousepress.com or call 866-565-2900.

LIBRARY OF CONGRESS CATALOGING-IN-PUBLICATION DATA

Hillert, Margaret.
   Happy Easter, dear dragon / by Margaret Hillert; illustrated by Carl
Kock. — Rev. and expanded library ed.
      p. cm. — (Beginning to read series. Dear dragon)
   Summary: A boy and his pet dragon celebrate Easter by enjoying the
spring flowers and baby animals, coloring eggs, making an egg tree,
hunting for Easter eggs, marching in the Easter parade, and going to
church. Includes reading activities.
   ISBN-13: 978-1-59953-038-3 (library binding : alk. paper)
   ISBN-10: 1-59953-038-4 (library binding : alk. paper)
   [1. Easter—Fiction. 2. Dragons—Fiction.] I. Kock, Carl, ill.
II. Title. III. Series.
PZ7.H558Has 2007
[E]—dc22   2006007086

Oh, my. Oh, my.
Come out here.
Look at this
and this
and this.

What pretty ones.
See here and here and here.
Red, yellow and blue ones.

I can make something.
Something for you.
It is pretty.
Do you like it?

Now come with me.
Run, run, run.
I want you to see something.

Look here. Look here.
Little yellow balls.
Little yellow babies.

Come look here.
Look down in here.
Little babies are here, too.

And see this.
One, two, three babies.
I like the little babies.

Oh, oh.
What is this?
See it come down.
Run, run, run.

Look at that.
Do you see what I see?
It is pretty.
We can make something pretty, too.

13

Mother, Mother.
We want to do something.
Can you guess what?
Can you help us?

Yes, yes.
I can guess what you want.
And I can help.

Look here.
Here is what you want.
Now get to work.
You and Father get to work.
Work, work, work.

Oh, my.
How pretty.
What good work you do.

You can do this, too.
Come and do this.
You will have to work at it.

That is good.
My! How pretty it is.
I like it.

Now I have something.
Something for you two.
You have to find it.
Go and look for it.

Oh, Mother.
Here it is.
And it is good to eat, too.

Look at us now.
We look good.
It is fun to do this.

I will go in here.
You can not come,
but do not go away.
I will come out.

27

We can go now.
Here you are with me.
And here I am with you.
Oh, what a happy Easter, dear dragon.

The following activities support the findings of the National Reading Panel that determined the most effective components for reading instruction are: Phonemic Awareness, Phonics, Vocabulary, Fluency, and Text Comprehension.

Phonemic Awareness: The long e sound

Oddity Task: Say the long **e** (as in Easter) sound for your child. Ask your child to find and say any word that has the long **e** sound in the following word groups:

bee, bet, bin	man, mean, mom	dear, dirt, dart	fun, fan, funny
tent, top, tree	salt, seal, sent	hip, hop, happy	red, read, road

Phonics: The letter Ee

1. Demonstrate how to form the letters **E** and **e** for your child.
2. Have your child practice writing **E** and **e** at least three times each.
3. Ask your child to point to the words in the book that have the letter **e** in them.
4. Write the words listed below on separate pieces of paper. Read each word aloud and ask your child to repeat them.

dear	happy	Easter	family	baby
three	eat	pretty	read	meet
sleep	seat	silly	jeep	meat

5. Write the following long **e** spellings at the top of a piece of paper.

   ee   ea   y

6. Ask your child to sort the words by placing them under the correct long **e** spelling.

Vocabulary: Story Words

1. Write the following words on separate pieces of paper and point to them as you read them to your child:

flowers	chicks	ducklings	babies
eggs	hunt	basket	raindrops

30

2. Say the following sentences aloud and ask your child to point to the word that is described:
   - In the springtime, these plants bloom in pretty colors. (flowers)
   - These fall from the sky to help plants grow. (raindrops)
   - Spring is when many animals have their (babies).
   - Baby chickens are called (chicks).
   - Baby ducks are called (ducklings).
   - For Easter, we dye these in many different colors (eggs).
   - When you go looking for hidden eggs it is called an Easter egg (hunt).
   - When you find eggs on an Easter egg hunt, you can put them in a (basket).

Fluency: Echo Reading

1. Reread the story to your child at least two more times while your child tracks the print by running a finger under the words as they are read. Ask your child to read the words he or she knows with you.
2. Reread the story, stopping after each sentence or page to allow your child to read (echo) what you have read. Repeat echo reading and let your child take the lead.

Text Comprehension: Discussion Time

1. Ask your child to retell the sequence of events in the story.
2. To check comprehension, ask your child the following questions:
   - After it rained, what happened when the sun came out?
   - What do you think the people on page 24 and 25 are doing?
   - If your family celebrates Easter, ask: What do we do to celebrate Easter?
   - If your family does not celebrate Easter, ask: What special celebrations do we have in the spring? What do we do to celebrate?

WORD LIST

Happy Easter, Dear Dragon uses the 68 words listed below.
This list can be used to practice reading the words that appear in the text. You may wish to write the words on index cards and use them to help your child build automatic word recognition. Regular practice with these words will enhance your child's fluency in reading connected text.

a	Easter	I	oh	us
am	eat	in	one(s)	
and		is	out	want
are	father	it		we
at	find		pretty	what
away	for			will
	fun	like	red	with
babies		little	run	work
balls		look		
blue	get			
but	go	make	see	yellow
	good	me	something	yes
	guess	mother		you
can		my	that	
come	happy		the	
	help	not	this	
dear	here	now	three	
do	how		to	
down			too	
dragon			two	

ABOUT THE AUTHOR Margaret Hillert has written over 80 books for children who are just learning to read. Her books have been translated into many different languages and over a million children throughout the world have read her books. She first started writing poetry as a child and has continued to write for children and adults throughout her life. A first grade teacher for 34 years, Margaret is now retired from teaching and lives in Michigan where she likes to write, take walks in the morning, and care for her three cats.

Photograph by Glenna Washburn

ABOUT THE ADVISER Shannon Cannon contributed the activities pages that appear in this book. Shannon serves as a literacy consultant and provides staff development to help improve reading instruction. She is a frequent presenter at educational conferences and workshops. Prior to this she worked as an elementary school teacher and as president of a curriculum publishing company.